ISBN 1-84135-066-4

First published 2001 by Award Publications Limited,
27 Longford Street, London NW1 3DZ

Printed in Belgium

Paper Bears

The Very Beginning

by Sue Hall

AWARD PUBLICATIONS LIMITED

In a dusty attic full of things that nobody wanted, a little mouse climbed on top of a pretty teapot with a broken spout. As he sat there watching, the trapdoor opened and somebody pushed a brown paper bag up into the attic.

Inside it were two teddies that had belonged to a little boy and girl who lived in the house. But the children had grown up and no longer played with them.

The years passed and the bears were forgotten.

One evening the setting sun shone into the darkest corner of the attic, on to two furry heads peeping out of the crumpled brown paper bag with its label saying PAPER BEARS. Four eyes glowed with amber light. They belonged to Joshua and Tessie, the forgotten bears.

As it became dark, the first stars of the night started to shine outside. Above a tall fir-tree one star shone brighter than all the others. Her twinkling light came through the window and made the Paper Bears' eyes sparkle.

This was a magical star and her name was Twinkle. As the bears watched, she came down to peep through the attic window, dancing in the air outside it. Her starlight shone even brighter when she saw what she was looking for – the shiny glass eyes of the two forgotten teddy bears.

The window was not quite shut and Twinkle managed to slide through into the attic. She flew over to the Paper Bears and danced over their heads.

"Aaachoo," sneezed Joshua.

"Aaachoo," sneezed Tessie.

"Bless you," said Twinkle from inside a cloud of sparkling stardust.

The two bears climbed out of their paper bag and stretched their stiff arms and legs.

"Follow me," said Twinkle, settling on the windowsill.

Twinkle called to a fluffy little cloud which floated gently down from the sky and stopped by the window.

"Climb aboard," said Twinkle to the two bears. She sang a magic song, then off she flew, leading the way with the little cloud floating right behind her.

When the two bears felt brave enough to look down, they found they were floating over beautiful places. By the light of the moon they saw fairytale castles, snowy mountains and dark forests.

"Safe journey, little bears," called a small brown bear who was peeping out of a cave below.

They passed over brightly lit cities shining like jewels, over deep oceans and huge icebergs.

"Safe journey, little bears," called two baby polar bears, as snowflakes settled on the Paper Bears' heads.

Finally they saw the outline of an island.

"The Island of Forgotten Toys," said Twinkle with a smile.
Tessie and Joshua peered into the darkness as they
floated down on the cloud. Tessie was scared when she saw
strange tall shapes below them. Joshua was scared too. In
the moonlight he had seen lots of eyes peering up at them –
maybe there were hundreds of monsters here!

Twinkle told them not to be afraid because everyone here was friendly and it was a very beautiful place.

Tessie and Joshua held each other's paws tightly.

As soon as it became light the bears saw that they were standing on a long beach with blue sea lapping over yellow sand. Tessie realised that the scary shapes she had seen were only trees.

In front of them were many toys waiting to greet their new friends.

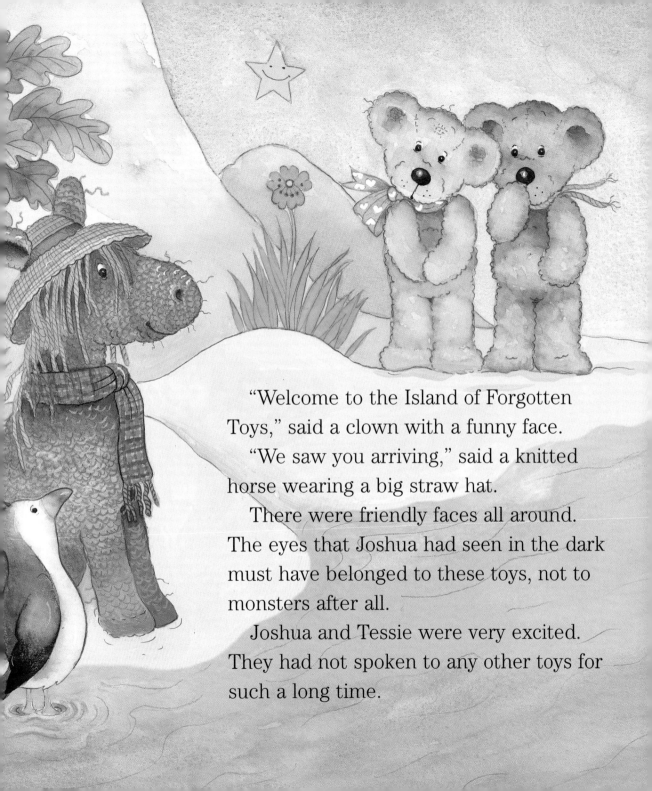

"Welcome to the Island of Forgotten Toys," said a clown with a funny face.

"We saw you arriving," said a knitted horse wearing a big straw hat.

There were friendly faces all around. The eyes that Joshua had seen in the dark must have belonged to these toys, not to monsters after all.

Joshua and Tessie were very excited. They had not spoken to any other toys for such a long time.

The two Paper Bears smiled and hugged each other. They were sure they would be very happy in their new home.

Joshua and Tessie thanked Twinkle
for rescuing them from the dark attic.
Twinkle smiled as she watched them
beginning to play with all the other
forgotten toys – their new friends.